THE LOST

MILK JAR

By Lucy Ann Conley
Artist: Edith Burkholder

Code no. 86-8-99
Catalog no. 2327
Printed in U.S.A.

Little
JEWEL
Books

Copyright 1986 by
Rod and Staff Publishers, Inc.
Crockett, Kentucky 41413

"Time to go for milk," called John. He sat on the floor to pull on his boots. "Come, David. Let's be the horses. Mother says it's time to go for milk."

"We want to go along," cried Beth, running for her coat. "Don't we, Sara?"

"Are we going to sled?" Sara asked eagerly.

"Yes, you may take the sled." Mother stooped to help Sara with her boots.

David finished buckling his boots. Then he followed John outdoors.

Together the boys pulled the sled up to the porch.

"Come on, Sara," David called, stomping his feet up and down in the soft snow. "Hurry, Beth. I'm a frisky horse!"

Beth sat down on the sled holding the gallon jar carefully. Sara sat behind her.

"Here we go!" shouted the boys.
The sled ran smoothly over the hard-packed
snowy lane.

Soon David and John slowed down.
"Now—I'm—a—tired—horse," David
puffed as they pulled the sled through the soft
snow at the side of the road.

The boys turned in the Smith's lane and pulled the sled up to the back porch.

Beth and Sara scrambled off the sled and followed the boys up to the door.

"Come in," Mrs. Smith called cheerily. "What rosy cheeks! It's cold outdoors, isn't it?"

Mrs. Smith took milk from the refrigerator and poured it into the jar.

Soon the children were on their way
home. Beth and Sara sat on the sled holding
the gallon jar of milk tightly. The boys
pulled the sled smoothly across the snow.

Then the boys began to run and John warned, "Hold on, girls!"

Beth clutched the milk jar in both arms, and Sara clung tightly to Beth. The sled skimmed lightly over the snowy lane.

"We're flying, we're flying!" sang Beth. They came to the end of the lane. Around the curve they flew, and the sled upset in a big soft snowbank.

"O-o-oh!" squealed Sara as she landed
headfirst in the snow.

Beth sat up in the middle of the snowbank,
laughing. Her mouth and eyes were full of
snow.

"Are you hurt?" John asked kindly, brushing the snow off Beth's face.

"No," both girls laughed. "We're all right."

David pulled the sled out of the snowbank.
"Where is the milk?" he wondered.
"The milk!" gasped Beth. "Did we lose
it?"

"I don't see it." David kicked into the snowbank with the toe of his boot.

John scooped snow away with his hands. There was no milk jar to be seen.

"It just isn't here," Beth said anxiously. "What will Mother say?"

"Let's ask God where the milk is," Sara
suggested.

The children knelt in the snow and bowed
their heads to pray. They asked God to help
them find the milk if it was His will.

Then they heard a soft *me-ow*.

Mrs. Smith's gray kitten had followed them to the road. Its little pink nose twitched as it sniffed eagerly at the snow.

"What do you smell, kitty?" John asked.
He walked over to see. "Our milk!" he cried
in surprise. "Look!"

The milk jar was buried in deep snow, but
a bit of the lid peeped out. Milk was leaking
out around the edge of the lid. That was what
the kitten wanted.

Me-ow! it pleaded.

"Oh, kitty," laughed David. "You found our lost milk!"

"Nice kitty," Beth said gently, stroking its soft fur.

"God made the kitty find the milk, didn't He?" Sara asked sweetly.

"Yes, He did, because we prayed," John replied. With a grunt he pulled the heavy milk jar from its hiding place.

David brushed the snow from the sled and
Sara and Beth sat down on the sled again.
John gave the milk jar to Beth who held it
tightly.

Away the boys ran. The sled skimmed
lightly over the snowy lane. The children
were hurrying home to tell Mother how the
Lord used the kitten to help them find the
lost milk jar.